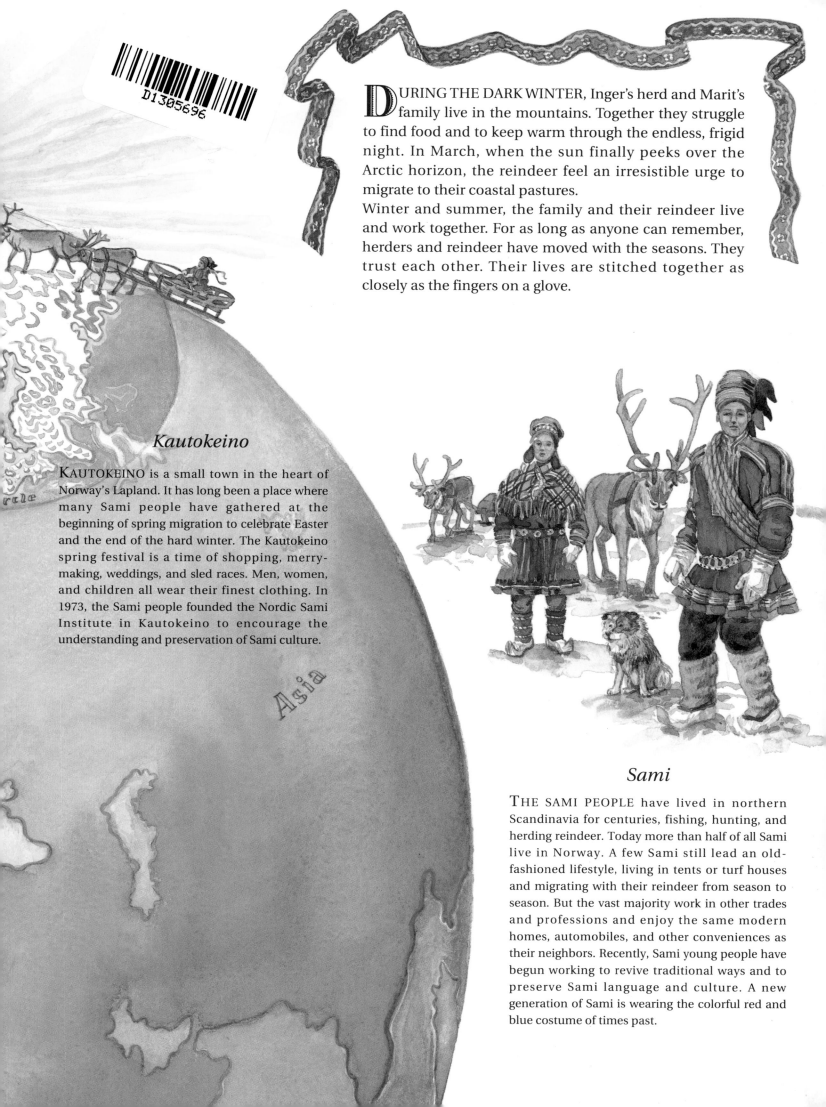

DURING THE DARK WINTER, Inger's herd and Marit's family live in the mountains. Together they struggle to find food and to keep warm through the endless, frigid night. In March, when the sun finally peeks over the Arctic horizon, the reindeer feel an irresistible urge to migrate to their coastal pastures.

Winter and summer, the family and their reindeer live and work together. For as long as anyone can remember, herders and reindeer have moved with the seasons. They trust each other. Their lives are stitched together as closely as the fingers on a glove.

Kautokeino

KAUTOKEINO is a small town in the heart of Norway's Lapland. It has long been a place where many Sami people have gathered at the beginning of spring migration to celebrate Easter and the end of the hard winter. The Kautokeino spring festival is a time of shopping, merry-making, weddings, and sled races. Men, women, and children all wear their finest clothing. In 1973, the Sami people founded the Nordic Sami Institute in Kautokeino to encourage the understanding and preservation of Sami culture.

Asia

Sami

THE SAMI PEOPLE have lived in northern Scandinavia for centuries, fishing, hunting, and herding reindeer. Today more than half of all Sami live in Norway. A few Sami still lead an old-fashioned lifestyle, living in tents or turf houses and migrating with their reindeer from season to season. But the vast majority work in other trades and professions and enjoy the same modern homes, automobiles, and other conveniences as their neighbors. Recently, Sami young people have begun working to revive traditional ways and to preserve Sami language and culture. A new generation of Sami is wearing the colorful red and blue costume of times past.

Inger's Promise

Written by **Jami Parkison**

Illustrated by **Andra Chase**

MarshMedia, Kansas City, Missouri

Dedicated to John Parkison, my most trustworthy friend.

Special thanks to Kate and Gabriel Parkison,
and Nettye Hugh Jones

Text © 1996 by Marsh Film Enterprises, Inc.

Illustrations © 1996 by Marsh Film Enterprises, Inc.

First Printing 1995
Second Printing 1997

Published by
        A Division of Marsh Film Enterprises, Inc.
        P. O. Box 8082
        Shawnee Mission, KS 66208

Library of Congress Cataloging-in-Publication Data
Parkison, Jami.
    Inger's promise/written by Jami Parkison; illustrated by Andra Chase.
        p.   cm.
    Summary: Inger, an ambitious young reindeer buck, finally proves
that he is reliable when the herd is surprised by a spring snowstorm in
the Lapland area of Norway.
    ISBN 1-55942-080-4
    [1. Reindeer—Fiction. 2. Sami (European people)—Fiction.
3. Norway—Fiction. 4. Reliability—Fiction.] I. Chase, Andra, ill. II. Title.
PZ7.P2394In 1996   95-34472
[E]—dc20

Book layout by Cirrus Design

Printed in Hong Kong

Reindeer bells jingled in the frosty air. Snow drifts lined the sidewalks in spiny rows.
"It's a white wonderland, Inger," said Marit. The girl looped her arm around the
reindeer's neck.

In all the world, Inger was sure no place rivaled Kautokeino, Norway. Fancy shops
filled the mountain town's main street: sled-builders, ski-outfitters, silversmiths, craft-
makers, bakers. Brightly dressed herders and their prized reindeer streamed into town.

"Boriz!" they greeted each other.

Kautokeino was the first stop on the herders' annual migration to coastal pastures,
and it was Spring Festival, a time to celebrate the end of the long polar night.

Looking out over the festival streets, Inger determined to make the most of the
holiday. And what better way to begin the festivities than by going to a wedding!

Marit's older sister was getting married.

"And guess what, Inger!" Marit said, as she led the reindeer to the sled-builder's shop. "You're invited. You'll pull the bride and groom's sled to the reception. I told Father you're the perfect choice—with your white fur and your antlers."

"What an honor, Inger!" said Midnight Sun.

"Inger's antlers are quite magnificent," said Dot. She was Midnight Sun's daughter, and like other one-year-olds, Dot greatly admired the handsome Inger.

"Fancy fur and a mountain of antlers aren't enough," said Old Moss, the herd's oldest reindeer. "Weddings are important, so you must be reliable. You're still young—"

"Young, yes," interrupted Inger, "but absolutely reliable. You can count on me!"

Wearing bright pompoms and silver bells, Inger stood near the church doors, harnessed to the brand-new sled. Waiting for the bride and groom, Inger daydreamed about the sled ride to the reception. He imagined . . .

artisans carving his likeness in ice . . .

photographers snapping each perfect prance . . .

journalists reporting the whole Triumphant Journey.

Suddenly, the doors opened and the wedding party stepped out. A breeze lifted the bride's filmy veil. It fluttered across Inger's face and tickled his nose.

Inger arched his neck and snagged the flapping veil with his antlers. The veil lifted from the bride's head. Inger shook his antlers and whirled about madly. Soon the white veil encircled Inger's head like a mountain fog.

At last Aslak, Marit's brother, lassoed Inger's antlers and wrestled him to the ground.

For the rest of the festival week, Inger was too embarrassed to talk to anyone.

        Every whisper,

              every giggle,

                      every sideways glance—

Inger was sure they were all aimed at him. How would he ever make up for the wedding-day disaster?

Inger's chance soon came.

"We need a reindeer for the Alta River Sled Race," announced Midnight Sun.

Inger pushed his way through the gathering of reindeer. "Choose me," he said.

Midnight Sun frowned. Inger knew she was remembering the wedding veil. "I'm not very good at waiting," he admitted, "but this is a race. I can run fast as the wind."

Midnight Sun conceded. "Everyone deserves a second chance—but remember, we're depending on you."

"You can count on me!" promised Inger.

Each family had entered its best reindeer for the sprint down the ice-covered river. Aslak strapped Inger's harness to the sled and climbed aboard.

"On your mark!" shouted Marit's father. "Get set! GO!"

Inger dashed from the starting line like a blazing comet.

The crowd shouted. Herd dogs barked. Inger thought he heard Marit's voice whooping excitedly, "Faster!"

Inger pulled ahead. His heart pounded. Whish, whish, went the sleds as they rocketed down the track. "Dragging a sled at break-neck speed is hard work," thought Inger.

Just then something sailed across Inger's path.

It was a snowy owl. The bird blinked its yellow eyes, tipped its wings in greeting, and then glided away. Inger bounded after the owl, forgetting all about the race and the crowd—and his promise.

The next day, when the family packed to leave Kautokeino, Marit's father tied Inger to the back of his sled. "This will keep you out of trouble," he said.

Old Moss shook his head solemnly at the humiliated Inger.

"You're just not trustworthy," explained Midnight Sun.

While he trudged along, tethered behind the sled, Inger remembered Midnight Sun's words. When he was finally released, he headed straight for the outer edge of the migrating herd, where he remained, a solitary reindeer.

Late one afternoon, the sky filled with dark clouds. They rolled in on top of each other, lower and lower, until they hung overhead like a box lid. By dusk, snow fell thick as pillow feathers.

Inger wandered blindly through the spring storm. Hoping to find shelter under pine trees, he pushed his way through the branches. Inside the sanctuary he found Old Moss and Dot.

"The herd is scattered," said Inger.

"We'll have to go on by ourselves," Old Moss replied.

"Inger will lead us," Dot said brightly.

Old Moss' face darkened. He said nothing, but Inger knew what he was thinking. Nobody trusted Inger any more.

"I'll get us to the coast," Inger said firmly. "You can count on me."

And so began Inger's longest journey.

The journey was perilous.
    Hidden crevices threatened each step.
        Bears and wolves prowled the migratory route.
But Inger kept the three reindeer together, safe.

One day they stood before a wide, turbulent river. Only Inger had the strength to swim across.

He made two trips—first carrying Dot and then Old Moss, who climbed on Inger's back. Inger paddled furiously. Strong currents nearly dragged him under. Still Inger plowed steadily through the lashing river, until everyone stood safely on the opposite shore.

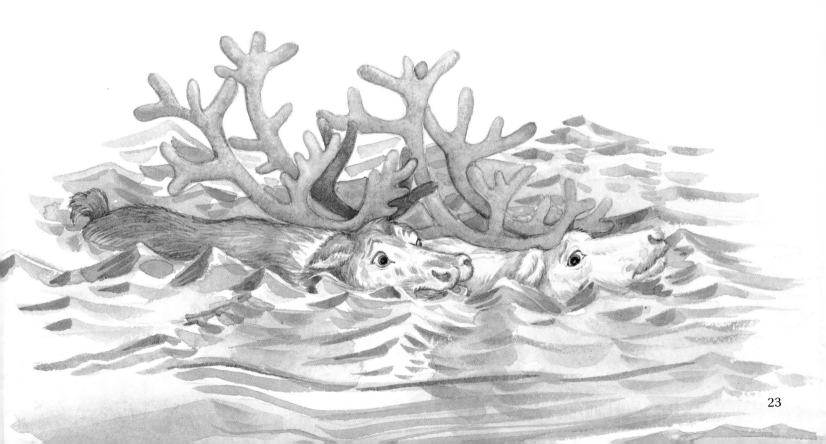

That night they rested under a stand of trees. Inger was tired, and every muscle ached. Inger knew he could make the treacherous trip to the coast by himself, but he wasn't sure he could make it if he had to continue traveling with Old Moss and Dot. Why did he have to travel with them? What if he left tonight, while they slept? What difference would it make?

Old Moss waited for Dot to fall asleep. "I doubted you'd keep your promise," he said to Inger. "Time and again, you've claimed we could count on you, but I had learned not to trust you. I was wrong, Inger. Now I believe you'll do your best to get us home."

Inger sighed. Old Moss and Dot believed in him. It was true that he could run away. But what wasn't true was that it didn't make any difference. It did. If he didn't keep his promise, it would make all the difference in the world to Dot and Old Moss.

The next morning, Old Moss and Dot dug for lichens near a birch grove. Not far away, Inger searched for food by some rocks. Suddenly, Inger pricked up his ears and sniffed. When he looked back at the birches, the fur along his back bristled.

A wolf had cornered Old Moss and Dot.

Old Moss stepped forward, trying to block the wolf's path to Dot. Spooked by the movement, the wolf hunched his shoulders, ready to attack. Every instinct told Inger to run, but he knew Old Moss and Dot could not fight off the wolf alone.

Inger banged his antlers against a rock. The wolf spun around, his narrow eyes gauging Inger. Inger lowered his head. His long, handsome antlers pointed like an army of spears.

Inger lunged. Dodging the attack, the wolf snapped at Inger's leg. Inger kicked the wolf's neck. With his sharp teeth, the wolf grabbed the reindeer's side. Inger staggered backward, dragging the wolf with him. In a furious ball of snow and fur, the two animals tumbled to the ground.

When they finally stood apart, Inger lunged again. Using his antlers, he tossed the wolf against a boulder, then charged forward, pressing his antlers into the rock. The trick worked. The wolf was pinned inside an antler cage.

And then, with a splintering crack, one of Inger's antlers broke off.

Seizing the chance to escape, the startled wolf ran away, yelping.

Side by side by side, three tired reindeer stood on summer pastures, which spread out before them like a green quilt. In the distance, the herd grazed tranquilly, and a reassuring curl of smoke rose from the chimney of the family's hut. As if to welcome the lost reindeer, the twilight blazed with the aurora borealis, a dazzling display of yellow and green lights.

The long journey was over. Inger had kept his promise.

Someone ran from the hut. "Boriz, Inger!" called Marit, both arms waving.

Midnight Sun reached the lost reindeer first.

"Inger brought us home," announced Old Moss.

Midnight Sun nodded toward Inger's head. "The journey cost you an antler," she said.

"It'll grow back," said Inger, and trotted off to Marit.

Old Moss and Dot looked at each other and smiled. "You can count on it."

Dear Parents and Educators:

Researchers have documented that success in life depends more upon successful relationships than upon specific academic or vocational skills. Family units thrive with members who are sensitive to each other's needs, practice cooperation, and work together to solve problems. And employers are realizing that people who initiate and support positive interpersonal relationships are an asset in the workplace.

Inger's story reminds children and adults that trust is one of the most important ingredients in building strong relationships. For most youngsters, being reliable and dependable takes effort and determination. Boys and girls rely on good modeling and practice to fine tune their behaviors. When adults are in the habit of doing what they say they are going to do, children see that verbal commitments do translate into actions. They learn that they too can develop more secure relationships if they are responsible for their own words and behaviors. As children grow and are challenged with age-appropriate responsibilities, they learn to have confidence in themselves, and this also helps them to build trust into their relationships. There are many personal rewards as young people practice and develop reliability. When they are treated as trustworthy, they feel valuable, capable, and significant in their relationships. Then the phrase "You can count on me!" becomes more that just words. It becomes an enthusiastic statement of intent to back up words with action!

Encourage children to share their ideas and feelings about Inger's experiences. Here are some questions you might ask to initiate discussion about the message of *Inger's Promise:*

✻ Who are Inger's friends?

✻ What were some of the problems that Inger had in the story?

✻ Who "caused" these problems?

✻ What could Inger have done differently to avoid these problems?

✻ When Inger said, "You can count on me," did his friends believe him?

✻ How did Inger feel when his behavior did not support his words?

✻ What did Inger have to do to show that he was trustworthy?

✻ Can you recall a time when you behaved in a dependable way?

✻ Did anyone notice?

✻ How did you feel about your behavior?

Available from MarshMedia

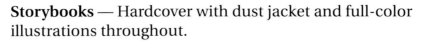

Storybooks — Hardcover with dust jacket and full-color illustrations throughout.

Videos — The original story and illustrations combined with dramatic narration, music, and sound effects.

Activity Books — Softcover collections of games, puzzles, maps, and project ideas designed for each title.

Amazing Mallika, written by Jami Parkison, illustrated by Itoko Maeno. 32 pages. ISBN 1-55942-087-1. Video. 15:05 run time. ISBN 1-55942-088-X.

Bailey's Birthday, written by Elizabeth Happy, illustrated by Andra Chase. 32 pages. ISBN 1-55942-059-6. Video. 18:00 run time. ISBN 1-55942-060-X.

Bea's Own Good, written by Linda Talley, illustrated by Andra Chase. 32 pages. ISBN 1-55942-092-8. Video. 15:00 run time. ISBN 1-55942-093-6.

Clarissa, written by Carol Talley, illustrated by Itoko Maeno. 32 pages. ISBN 1-55942-014-6. Video. 13:00 run time. ISBN 1-55942-023-5.

Gumbo Goes Downtown, written by Carol Talley, illustrated by Itoko Maeno. 32 pages. ISBN 1-55942-042-1. Video. 18:00 run time. ISBN 1-55942-043-X.

Hana's Year, written by Carol Talley, illustrated by Itoko Maeno. 32 pages. ISBN 1-55942-034-0. Video. 17:10 run time. ISBN 1-55942-035-9.

Inger's Promise, written by Jami Parkison, illustrated by Andra Chase. 32 pages. ISBN 1-55942-080-4. Video. 18:00 run time. ISBN 1-55942-081-2.

Jomo and Mata, written by Alyssa Chase, illustrated by Andra Chase. 32 pages. ISBN 1-55942-051-0. Video. 20:00 run time. ISBN 1-55942-052-9.

Kiki and the Cuckoo, written by Elizabeth Happy, illustrated by Andra Chase. 32 pages. ISBN 1-55942-038-3. Video. 14:30 run time. ISBN 1-55942-039-1.

Kylie's Concert, written by Patty Sheehan, illustrated by Itoko Maeno. 32 pages. ISBN 1-55942-046-4. Video. 17:20 run time. ISBN 1-55942-047-2.

Kylie's Song, written by Patty Sheehan, illustrated by Itoko Maeno. 32 pages. (Advocacy Press) ISBN 0-911655-19-0. Video. 12:00 run time. ISBN 1-55942-021-9.

Minou, written by Mindy Bingham, illustrated by Itoko Maeno. 64 pages. (Advocacy Press) ISBN 0-911655-36-0. Video. 18:30 run time. ISBN 1-55942-015-4.

Molly's Magic, written by Penelope Colville Paine, illustrated by Itoko Maeno. 32 pages. ISBN 1-55942-068-5. Video. 16:00 run time. ISBN 1-55942-069-3.

My Way Sally, written by Mindy Bingham and Penelope Paine, illustrated by Itoko Maeno. 48 pages. (Advocacy Press) ISBN 0-911655-27-1. Video. 19:30 run time. ISBN 1-55942-017-0.

Papa Piccolo, written by Carol Talley, illustrated by Itoko Maeno. 32 pages. ISBN 1-55942-028-6. Video. 18:00 run time. ISBN 1-55942-029-4.

Pequeña the Burro, written by Jami Parkison, illustrated by Itoko Maeno. 32 pages. ISBN 1-55942-055-3. Video. 16:45 run time. ISBN 1-55942-056-1.

Plato's Journey, written by Linda Talley, illustrated by Itoko Maeno. 32 pages. ISBN 1-55942-100-2. Video. 15:00 run time. ISBN 1-55942-101-0.

Tessa on Her Own, written by Alyssa Chase, illustrated by Itoko Maeno. 32 pages. ISBN 1-55942-064-2. Video. 14:00 run time. ISBN 1-55942-065-0.

Time for Horatio, written by Penelope Paine, illustrated by Itoko Maeno. 48 pages. (Advocacy Press) ISBN 0-911655-33-6. Video. 19:00 run time. ISBN 1-55942-026-X.

Tonia the Tree, written by Sandy Stryker, illustrated by Itoko Maeno. 32 pages. (Advocacy Press) ISBN 0-911655-16-6. Video. 12:10 run time. ISBN 1-55942-019-7.

You can find storybooks at better bookstores. Or you may order storybooks, videos, and activity books direct by calling MarshMedia toll free at 1-800-821-3303.

MarshMedia has been publishing high-quality, award-winning learning materials for children since 1969. To receive a free catalog, call 1-800-821-3303.

Arctic Circle

THE ARCTIC CIRCLE is an imaginary line encircling the region that surrounds the North Pole. Lapland lies north of this line. The winters in Sami territory are long and cold. Snow may cover the ground for more than half the year, and temperatures stay below 0°F much of the time. Because of the tilt of the earth on its axis as it moves around the sun, people living north of the Arctic Circle have very long nights in the winter and very long days in the summer. In fact, in midwinter the sun is not seen for weeks, and at midsummer it never sets entirely. The area north of the Arctic Circle is sometimes called the land of the midnight sun.

Lapland and Norway

LAPLAND is not a country. It is a region that runs across several countries—Finland, Sweden, Russia, and Norway—above the Arctic Circle. Lapland is the home of the Sami (Lapp) people, the reindeer herders. Inger's story takes place in the part of Lapland at the top of the Kingdom of Norway, a sparsely populated, mountainous country, whose capital is Oslo.

caribou

Reindeer

IN PREHISTORIC TIMES, reindeer crossed the ice-packed land bridge that then connected Alaska and Asia, making their way across Siberia and into Europe. (Their relatives who remained in North America are called caribou.) In time reindeer were domesticated by the Sami people, who depended upon them for food and the materials for clothing, shelter, and tools. Reindeer are group animals. They stay in herds, migrating along well-established routes as the seasons change. In winter, the reindeer dig through the snow to uncover lichen, also called reindeer moss. During the warmer months, they are able to add berries, leaves, and other vegetation to their diets. Reindeer are about three feet high at the shoulder. Both males and females have large, branching antlers that can be used for defense or attack. The broad hooves of reindeer help them to travel over ice and snow. Their loosely-connected anklebones make a clicking sound as they walk or run.